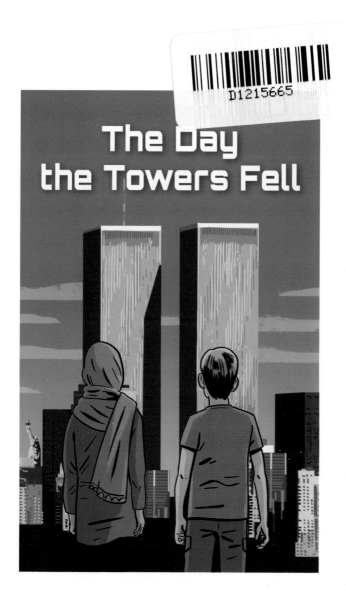

The Day
the Towers Fell

By Heather E. Schwartz
Illustrated by Chris King

Publishing Credits

Rachelle Cracchiolo, M.S.Ed., *Publisher*
Conni Medina, M.A.Ed., *Editor in Chief*
Nika Fabienke, Ed.D., *Content Director*
Véronique Bos, *Creative Director*
Shaun N. Bernadou, *Art Director*
Susan Daddis, M.A.Ed., *Editor*
John Leach, *Assistant Editor*
Jess Johnson, *Graphic Designer*

Image Credits

Illustrated by Chris King

Library of Congress Cataloging-in-Publication Data

Names: Schwartz, Heather E., author. | King, Chris (Illustrator),
 illustrator.
Title: The day the towers fell / by Heather Schwartz ; illustrated by Chris
 King. Description: Huntington Beach, CA : Teacher Created Materials, [2020] |
 Includes book club questions. | Audience: Age 12. | Audience: Grades
 4-6.
Identifiers: LCCN 2019026021 (print) | LCCN 2019026022 (ebook) | ISBN
 9781644913413 (paperback) | ISBN 9781644914311 (electronic)
Subjects: LCSH: Readers (Elementary) | September 11 Terrorist Attacks,
 2001--Juvenile fiction. | September 11 Terrorist Attacks, 2001--Comic
 books, strips, etc. | Time travel--Juvenile fiction. | Time
 travel--Comic books, strips, etc. | Graphic novels.
Classification: LCC PE1119 .S445 2020 (print) | LCC PE1119 (ebook) | DDC
 428.6/2--dc23
LC record available at https://lccn.loc.gov/2019026021
LC ebook record available at https://lccn.loc.gov/2019026022

Teacher Created Materials

5301 Oceanus Drive
Huntington Beach, CA 92649-1030
www.tcmpub.com

ISBN 978-1-6449-1341-3

The events of September 11, 2001, happened before I was born. We never learned much about it in school before now.

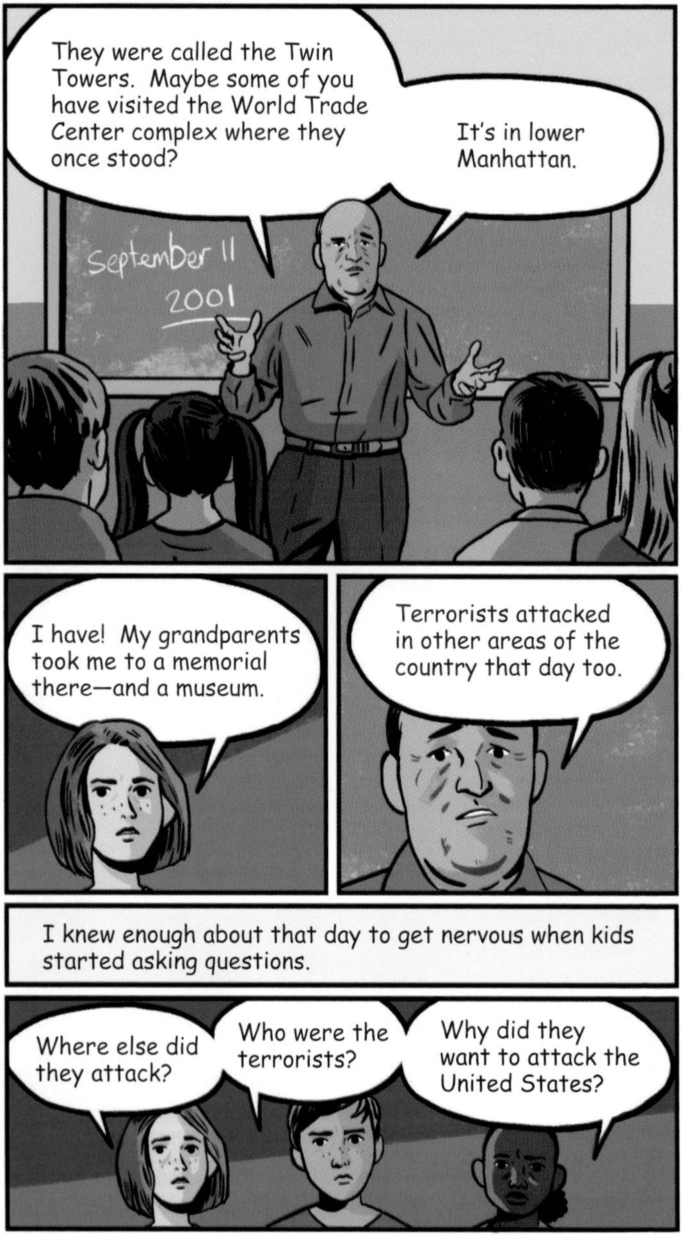
They were called the Twin Towers. Maybe some of you have visited the World Trade Center complex where they once stood?
It's in lower Manhattan.
September 11 2001
I have! My grandparents took me to a memorial there—and a museum.
Terrorists attacked in other areas of the country that day too.
I knew enough about that day to get nervous when kids started asking questions.
Where else did they attack?
Who were the terrorists?
Why did they want to attack the United States?

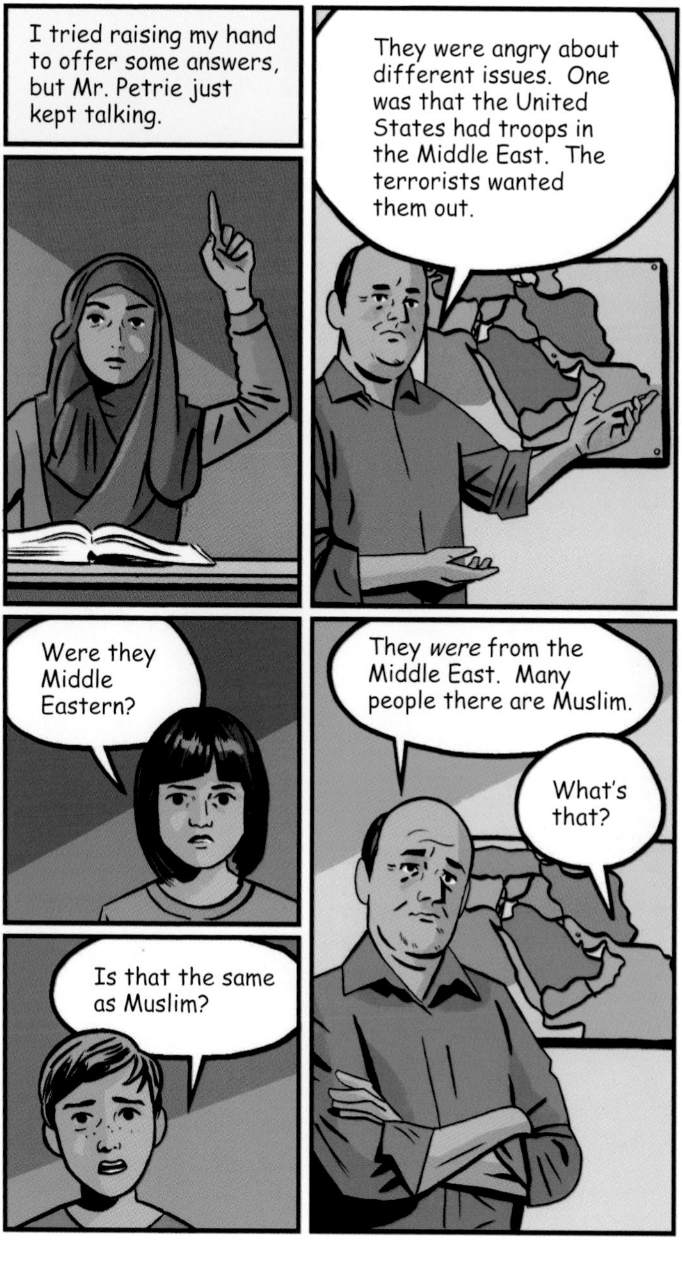
I tried raising my hand to offer some answers, but Mr. Petrie just kept talking.
They were angry about different issues. One was that the United States had troops in the Middle East. The terrorists wanted them out.
Were they Middle Eastern?
They *were* from the Middle East. Many people there are Muslim.
What's that?
Is that the same as Muslim?

I shrunk down in my seat when Mr. Petrie started to explain. And for a teacher, he wasn't doing an excellent job—probably a C– at best. As he talked, kids were looking over at me.

Muslims are people who follow Islam, the religion. The men who planned the attacks were Muslim, but they were also terrorists.

They belonged to a group called al-Qaeda and planned the attacks.

What is a terrorist?

A terrorist is someone who uses fear or violence to try to make a change.

I raised my hand again, hoping to explain a little better how the Muslims they know are different from terrorists. But Mr. Petrie didn't call on me.

Finally, the bell rang, and class was over at last! But in the hall, the questions kept coming—except now they were directed at me.

The headscarves are a Muslim thing, right?

Do you ever get scared people might think you're a terrorist?

Do your parents know your religion has terrorists in it?

Hey, don't be so rude—Sari's not a terrorist!

Well duh, *I* know that. I'm just saying, *people*.

Walking home, I felt exposed and noticeable in a way I never had before.

Why had I chosen such a bright hijab to wear that day?

Was everyone who passed by in their cars looking at me?

At dinner, I talked to my parents about what had happened. They didn't seem to think it was an issue.

So today, we talked about September 11. Everybody started asking me dumb questions. I wish I wasn't the only Muslim kid in my class!

It's not so bad to be different.

Yes, it is! Especially when everyone thinks I'm different in a bad way!

This is a learning opportunity, Sari. You probably have a lot you can teach your classmates about our religion.

The next day was the anniversary of September 11, and I dreaded going back to school. I didn't even get a peaceful bus ride there.

Hey, Sari, I didn't mean to make you feel weird yesterday.

Oh...that's OK...

I was just wondering about stuff, and you're the only Muslim person I've ever met. So, I figured you might understand why Muslim people would want to attack the United States.

No, it's not like that! Those people were terror—

My voice was cut off by the ear-splitting sound of metal crushing metal. The bus jolted sideways. We screamed as backpacks, musical instruments, and kids fell off their seats into the aisle. We were in a crash! Andrew grabbed my hand and pulled me up off the floor.

Sari! Are you alright?

I think so...What's happening, though? We're in the wrong town or something.

Out the window, everything looked strange and unfamiliar.

Even the bus driver was wrong—a stranger was sitting in the seat usually occupied by Mrs. Karch.

If you kids are getting off here, come on and hurry up now.

Is that...Are those the Twin Towers?

You know it! If that's where you're headed, just walk a few blocks this way and you'll get to the World Trade Center in no time. Those towers are 110 stories high— can't miss 'em.

But I thought they were...wait—we're in New York City?

Now you're scaring me!

Yes, you're in lower Manhattan. A lot of people have to get to work right now, so please hurry up!

I glanced behind me and saw a line of people waiting to disembark. A woman wearing a hijab smiled at me, and even though everything was weird and confusing, I suddenly felt comforted instead of scared.

Just then, a shadow darkened the sky overhead and when I looked up, I saw a gigantic plane flying lower than I'd ever seen.

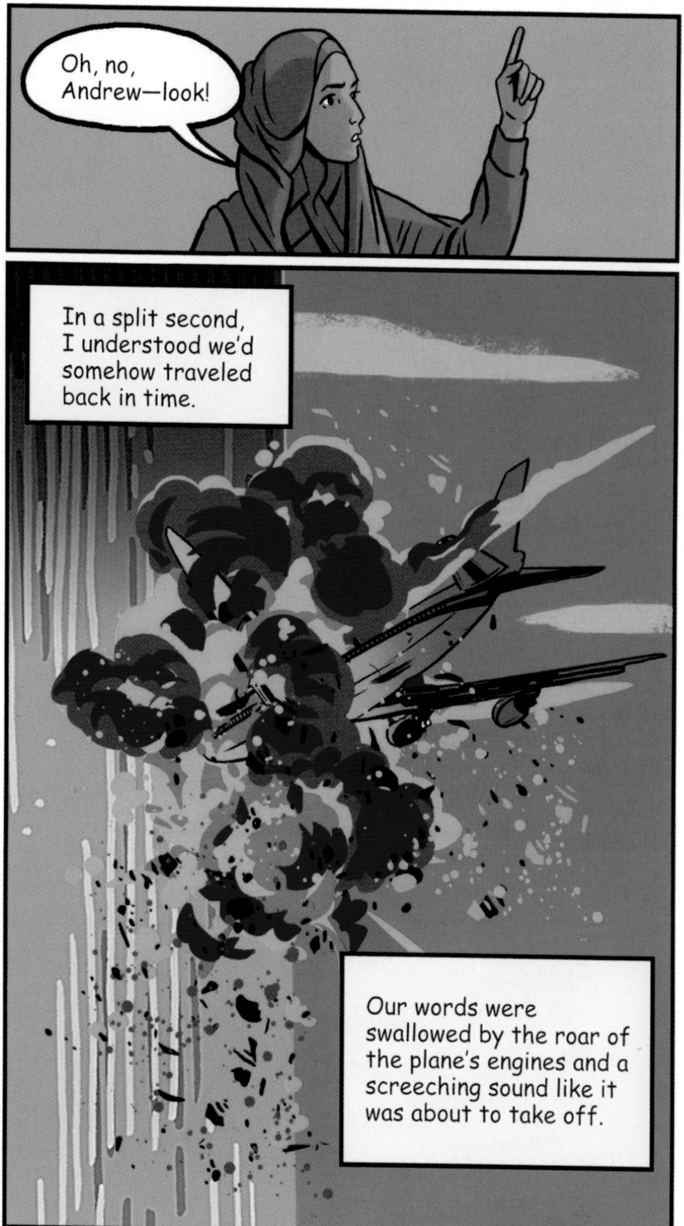
Oh, no, Andrew—look!
In a split second, I understood we'd somehow traveled back in time.
Our words were swallowed by the roar of the plane's engines and a screeching sound like it was about to take off.

We've got to get out of here!

This way!

We ran from the dust and debris. Then we heard a crash—the second plane! A policeman pointed us toward a bodega.

It's not safe here either!

We both knew what was coming next—the towers would fall soon too. So, we ran outside and joined the mob, running as fast as we could to try to escape the area.

Finally, we were far enough away from the dust and smoke to catch our breath and rest for a minute.

Then, we saw them and knew we had to help.

I was babysitting with my friend when the planes hit, but we got split up and now it's just me trying to get all these kids to safety!

Come on, follow me!

It's a race, and I bet I'm going to win!

I'll be the caboose so we don't lose anybody. See all that smoke? Let's pretend we're running away from a dragon!

I tried not to flinch when a big hunk of metal landed behind us. We still weren't moving very quickly, but if we could just keep going, I was sure we'd all make it out of here safely. I couldn't die on September 11, 2001— I had a life to live in the future!

It wasn't long before we ran into some other people. They had torn clothes and dirty faces.

One man's thawb was ripped down the side, and I glanced over at Andrew, worried he might notice the man was Muslim and be angry or afraid. But Andrew was smiling and handing the man a child to carry.

We made it to a school where a police officer told us it was safe to wait inside for our families.

We should go in, right? It's safer in there than it is out here on the street.

Of course! Although...we know more about what's going on than everyone else. This is history to us, so at least we know the attacks are over.

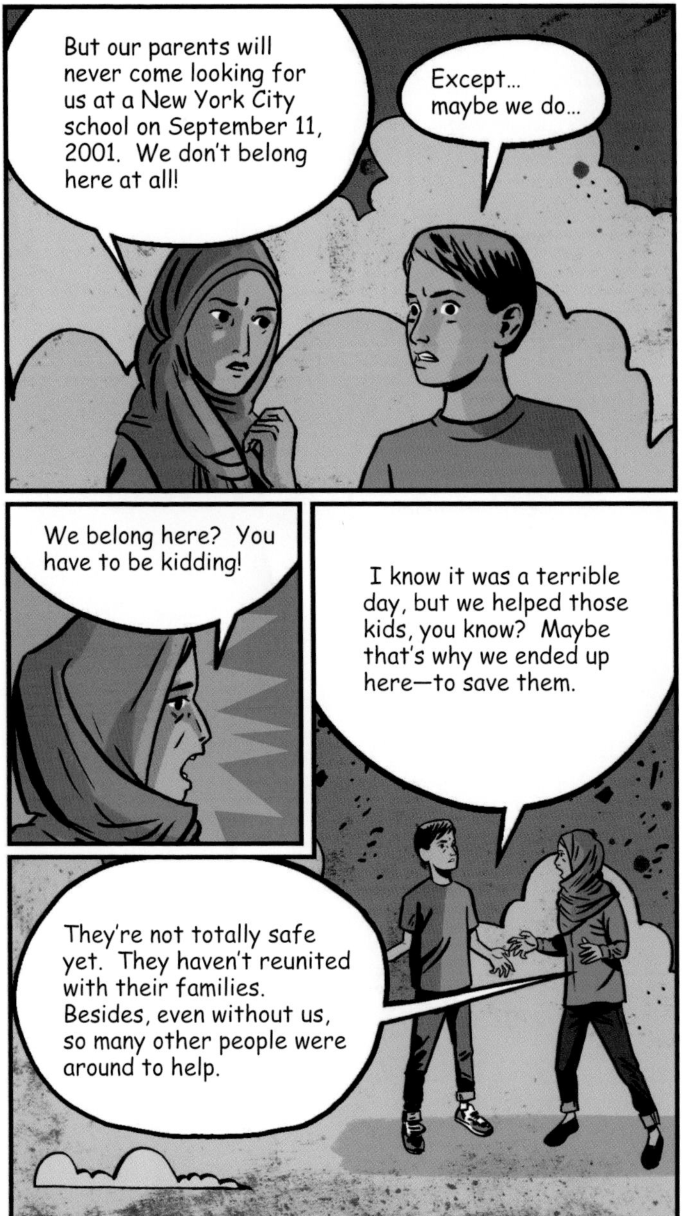

But our parents will never come looking for us at a New York City school on September 11, 2001. We don't belong here at all!
Except... maybe we do...
We belong here? You have to be kidding!
I know it was a terrible day, but we helped those kids, you know? Maybe that's why we ended up here—to save them.
They're not totally safe yet. They haven't reunited with their families. Besides, even without us, so many other people were around to help.

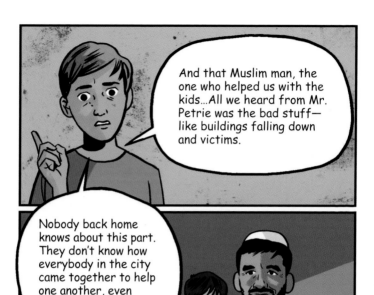

And that Muslim man, the one who helped us with the kids...All we heard from Mr. Petrie was the bad stuff—like buildings falling down and victims.

Nobody back home knows about this part. They don't know how everybody in the city came together to help one another, even though they were all different...and scared...

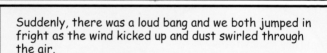

Suddenly, there was a loud bang and we both jumped in fright as the wind kicked up and dust swirled through the air.

BANG

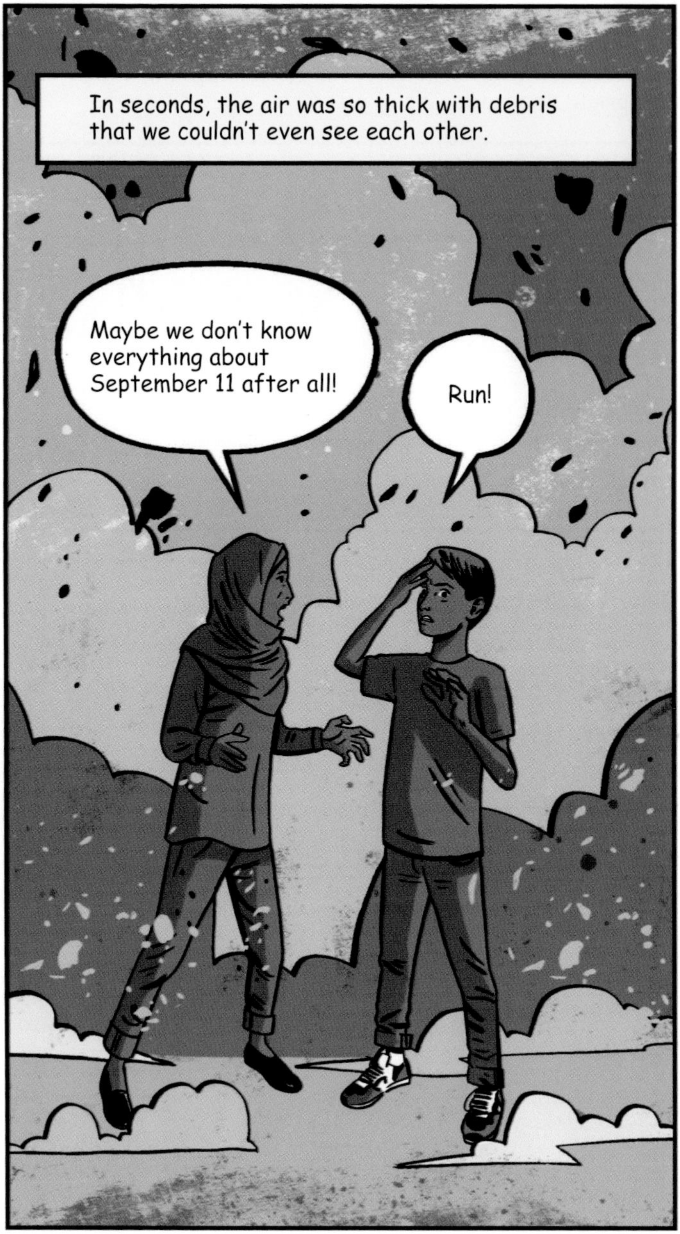
In seconds, the air was so thick with debris that we couldn't even see each other.
Maybe we don't know everything about September 11 after all!
Run!

As the dust settled and disappeared, I heard a low hum. I realized I was seated on the school bus, which was upright and moving along just fine.

I couldn't speak, but I pulled my phone out of my pocket and searched the internet.

I found what I was hoping for: an old newspaper article from 2001.

The following week, Andrew and I gave an awesome report on September 11 in school. The only problem was when Mr. Petrie asked for our sources. We didn't have any way of proving everything we wrote about.

But we both agreed a B was a pretty good grade.

A few weeks after that, we moved on to new subjects. We began studying internment camps. They were set up during World War II.

In the back of the room, I saw Yumi looking sad and worried. She was the only Japanese American person in our class. And then I noticed something else. Jamal was the only African American kid.

We were all different, but we were all part of this class. When we study something big, we all have something to say, we all have something to learn.

While Mr. Petrie announced we'd have another report due soon, I caught Andrew's eye and nodded at Yumi. I could tell he understood my meaning.

Can we do something different for this report? Maybe we could have the whole class work together somehow?

Well, that seems like a difficult way to work, with so many different people involved...

But that's why it would be awesome— we all have different ideas we can add!

My dad emigrated here. That might be relevant.

My grandpa fought in World War II.

Wow, really? It would be interesting to hear his story.

Mr. Petrie agreed that the class could work together. In the hall after class, Yumi wasn't the center of attention like I'd been after our lesson about 9/11. Instead, she headed to her next class while I stayed behind and talked to Andrew.

About Us

The Author

Heather E. Schwartz is the author of more than 100 nonfiction children's books. On September 11, 2001, she arrived in New York City minutes after the first plane hit the World Trade Center. It was a scary day, but in the months afterward, the people who lived and worked there looked out for each other. That made the city feel friendly and safe.

The Illustrator

From an early age, Chris King has taken inspiration from comic books, and some of his earliest memories are of copying pages of *Asterix the Gaul* in colored crayons. The feeling he gets from drawing with a pencil on paper is like no other. He has a degree in media production, specializing in animation and character design. Music is always playing when he's working.